The Woman who Read Romantic Fiction

And other stories

Helen Aileen Davies

Copyright © 2013 Helen Aileen Davies

Images Copyright © 2013 Robert Davies

The moral right of the author has been asserted.

Apart from any fair dealing for the purposes of research or private study, or criticism or review, as permitted under the Copyright, Design and Patents Act 1988, this publication may only be reproduced, stored or transmitted in any form or by any means, with the prior permission in writing of the author, or in the case of reprographic reproduction in accordance with the terms of licences issued by the Copyright Licensing Agency. Enquiries concerning reproduction outside of those terms should be sent to dragonfall@dragonfall.co.uk

Published by Dragonfall / Sweet Starling

ISBN: 978-0-9576328-0-6

Printed by Rainbow Print (Wales) Ltd.

With thanks to my parents, daughter and brother for their continuing support. With gratitude also to my wonderful husband Robert for his support and illustrations.

Diolch o galon i Cyril Jones am ei ysbridoliaeth.

Thanks also to

Jackie Askey, Chris Fawell and Paula Harcombe.

To Loris, Cinzia and all of the staff at the Hotel Nettunto, Bardolino without whom much of this book would never have been written. Their permission to use their names and weave them into the stories in the book is appreciated.

These stories are fictional:

any resemblance to persons living or dead is co-incidental.

Contents

The Woman Who Read Romantic Fiction 7

Her Father's Daughter 23

Marvelous Mrs Rushmore 51

The Ironing Lady 65

Status Change 81

The Bardolino Suite

The Maître D's Recommendation 97

The Safe Option 115

The Woman Who Read Romantic Fiction

The Woman Who Read Romantic Fiction

Kate stretched out her body under the warmth of the Mediterranean sun and dozed lazily. The blue sky above her seemed to reach out to caress the azure sea; the waves gently lapped the soft sparkling sand. Overhead the gulls called softly to each other. "Cacaw". Actually there was suddenly something distinctly un-gull-like about those calls. Blast. She fumbled to switch off the alarm and opened her eyes. Outside the rain was pouring. It seemed to have been raining for months. Ever since Jerry had left in fact. Jerry was her husband of 25 years who had walked out in the middle of their silver wedding anniversary dinner declaring that he "just couldn't do this any more" and had gone to live in a bed-sit with Polish office cleaner Anna, 20 years his junior. Kate wasn't sure what had hurt most, that he had left, that he left her for a girl barely older than their daughter, or that he made his announcement in public leaving her to clear up all the mess. Jerry had always had an interesting sense of timing. She turned on the shower letting the warm water cascade over her. Yes, it was Jerry who had chosen their wedding night to tell her how full of remorse he was after having had a one night stand with their bridesmaid. It was Jerry who sobbed begging for forgiveness on the day she came home from hospital with Ben, their second child – pacing the floor telling her that he would have no peace until he confessed his affair with their next door neighbour. It was Jerry who turned several odd shades of purple at parent's evening as they chatted to the young blonde teacher, only to later reveal that he had a brief fling with her when Kate was away looking after her mother. Why did she forgive him? Well, Jerry had a way of making her feel that it was all her fault in the first place. If she had not been so busy organising the wedding he wouldn't have felt neglected. If she hadn't been expecting Ben they would have had sex more often and he wouldn't have looked for comfort elsewhere. If she hadn't rushed to her mother's aid when she came out of hospital he wouldn't have been lonely. Secondly he displayed such anguish at his confessions, swearing his deepest love and devotion to her, telling her that he must have been mad, that there was no other woman in the world for him, that his very world would stop if she left him – so that by the time he laid his head childlike in her lap *she* was the one who felt guilty.

The Woman Who Read Romantic Fiction

At first she had longed for him acutely, but as the days passed she missed him more like one misses a persistent headache. Until, eventually, she found herself enjoying her own company. Her children and friends encouraged her to "get out there" but where "there" was she wasn't quite sure.

She dried herself and reached for the body lotion – budget version. This was not just because Jerry's income had gone. Two months after that bombshell she was told that there was to be some "re-organisation" at work, all of the P.A. jobs were being scrapped and the work was going to be handled by a "Central Administration Division" which would be more "efficient" and this meant that she would have to apply for a new job in the new "stream-lined" company. One month down the line it came as no surprise that no one over forty had been taken on. Her skills, shorthand, typing speeds, knowledge of how the company worked, were not needed in today's IT savvy office. The smart, short-skirted barely out of school temps were happy to take on the short term contracts with reduced pensions and no guarantees. Kate, and her colleagues, would be out of a job at the end of the month. She squeezed the last of the body lotion out of the bottle.

The Woman Who Read Romantic Fiction

She vaguely remembered a famous ex-supermodel on the TV telling everyone that she put cooking oil on her skin. Oh well, that would be it next month – eau de chips.

She looked at herself in the mirror. At forty three she was not looking too bad. Middle aged spread had not yet set in. There was no cellulite and not much in the way of wrinkles. In fact, she looked good – but that seemed to count for nothing. Once you had to scroll down the computer screen window for the year that you were born in, you were on the scrapheap - for everything it appeared.

Today was Friday. She had the day off to hunt for some jobs and to indulge her passion – the library. Kate loved to read and most of all she loved to read about love. She had fallen for Mr Darcy at the age of sixteen on the first reading of Pride and Prejudice and had swooned over those who came in his image through a thousand earnest romances, on the slopes of Italy, the deserts of Arabia, the jungles of Africa and New York – but all she had ever come home to was Jerry. And somehow or other, he had never managed to come a close second!

The Woman Who Read Romantic Fiction

She dressed, ate her toast, drank her cup of herbal tea and headed off in search of romance – fictional, that is.

Now the great problem with being an avid reader of romantic fiction is that the library doesn't always keep up. The stock was old and they didn't have the money to buy new books. It seemed to get harder each week to find something that she hadn't already read. She was currently romping through historical romance and this particular morning found herself straying into a set of shelves labelled "Historical Romantic Realism". Here were authors she had never read, Dostoevsky, Tolstoy, Zola – who on earth were they? Dickens she had heard of and had enjoyed adaptations of his stories in films and TV series. She had sat down and attempted to read his novels once – but for goodness sake he was so down right depressing! A happy ending – that was what she longed for.

What attracted her to these far flung volumes this morning however, was a pair of intelligent, but quizzical brown eyes, half hidden under tresses of unkempt brown hair and reading a novel by Emile Zola. He was too young, that much was obvious. A student, perhaps? The same sort of age as her son. And yet……. Despite herself she found her eyes tracing the line of his nose, straight, elegant, a *clever* sort of nose, and the curve of his face, a soft, sensitive sort of face. This would not do. What *was* the matter with her? Just as she recovered her composure he looked up and there was her composure all over the floor again!

"Ah" he whispered knowingly "A woman who reads. Do you like Zola?"

Like him? Up until five minutes ago Kate wasn't sure if he was a disinfectant or a sunflower oil. But the young man's voice was like rich hot chocolate and she was eager for another sip.

"Oh yes" she enthused. "One of my favourites!"

Was that her speaking? Well, it was her own voice that she heard. Thank goodness he had asked about one of the authors she could pronounce. How on earth did you say "Dostoevsky"?

"I love his realism, don't you?"

He really did have the most gorgeous eyes.

"Ermmm. Oh yes." Kate scanned the back of the book he was reading - "And of course….. his contribution to the ……French school of …….naturalistic fiction"

"Ah! That's it exactly! Where would they be – Maupassant, Camus – without Zola?"

"Where indeed" she agreed heartily. She really had to extricate herself from this conversation if only she could pull herself away from that perfect smile!

A low whirring noise came from his pocket.

"I'm late. Look, we're having a discussion group this evening at my place. Do you know 'The Avenue'?"

Kate nodded. It was the most expensive street in town.

"7 o'clock. Number 26." he began to rush off hurriedly putting his books down on the checkout counter. Kate watched as the clerk scanned the books. He was almost out of the door.

"Sebastian" he pointed a finger at his broad shoulders.

"Oh. Kate" she mouthed back.

The Woman Who Read Romantic Fiction

He waved and he was gone.

Of course she couldn't go. It would be ridiculous. Quite apart from the fact that he was hardly any older than her son, she knew absolutely nothing about French fiction. And even though she was a quick reader there was no way she was going to read even one of those novels by 7 that evening. Just as she was pondering her eye alighted on "French Literature –The Romantics". Could she perhaps cheat? What was she thinking of? The thought was preposterous! And even if she could blag her way through the evening, what on earth would she wear? Office suits would hardly do, evening dresses would be out of the question, yes she had jeans, but what to wear with them – a t-shirt would only emphasise her age, although a well cut blouse might do the trick. No this was silly. Put the book down and find some Georgette Heyer!

So it was, an hour later that she returned home with a baffling book on French literature in one hand and a Jaeger blouse bought in the sale in the other! She negotiated the long drive and now stood on the impressive doorstep of

"Number 26 The Avenue" trying hard to remember all that she had read that afternoon. Determinism, pessimism – surely there were more "isms" but just then Sebastian appeared at the door and she couldn't think of any of them. He waved her into the long lounge where a dozen eager faced students were debating earnestly.

"The whole essence can be traced back to Darwin" someone was saying.

Kate felt faint.

"Do you want a drink?"

Oh heaven - rescue!

She followed the pink-haired girl into the kitchen.

"Help yourself" – she pointed to an array of herbal teas, wine and glasses.

The debate in the adjoining room was heating up now. Try as she might she couldn't understand what they were talking about. Her heart began to gallop as if it was so ashamed of her it would run away. She suddenly felt old, awkward and stupid. The kitchen door was ajar. No one would notice if she made good her escape. She followed the garden path, her legs shaking. Silly foolish woman! What on earth did she think she was doing? She sat down heavily on a bench doing her best not to cry.

"Are you ok?"

She looked up. The sun was in her eyes. A tall man was standing over her. She thought at first that it was Sebastian, but then as her eyes adjusted to the light she saw that he was much older. He had the same kind eyes and sensitive face but the hair was shorter and greying slightly at the temples.

"Can I get you a glass of water?"

She nodded feebly. If she had tried to speak the tears would have flowed freely. She had made such a fool of herself. The sun was warm on her skin and the sweet scent of the nearby honeysuckle wafted on the air, but nothing could make her feel better. He returned with the water. Kate sipped it gratefully. He waited, watching her carefully.

"Are you Kate?" he asked.

"Yes." she answered, puzzled that he should know her name.

"I'm Jonathan. I must apologise for my son." He sat down beside her. His presence was soothing. Kate felt the throbbing in her head subside.

"Your son? Ah yes." The resemblance was obvious now. He turned to look at her and smiled. The corners of his eyes crinkled up and made her want to smile too.

"I'm sorry. When my wife died two years ago, I was broken-hearted. Sebastian worries about me – he thinks I am lonely. Perhaps he's right….. Anyway … he keeps trying to find a suitable girlfriend for me …a woman who reads." He shook his head. "He really had no right to ask you here without stating his intent. I am really sorry."

This was awkward.

Now the pieces fell together. Of course Sebastian wasn't interested in her. She felt - relieved.

"Why a woman who reads?" she enquired with a half-smile.

"I'm a professor of literature." He gave a wry grin back. She liked that smile.

"And are you a fan of Zola?" she asked falteringly.

He laughed loudly.

"He wouldn't be my first choice for something I want to read in my spare time."

His eyes twinkled. She liked those eyes. There was something warm, friendly and actually very sexy about him.

"Oh I'm so glad you said that! I didn't understand a word!" she was laughing too.

So they sat in the sun talking about books. Although he was an academic Kate had a pleasant surprise when he said he had read the odd Georgette Heyer himself. And as he spoke she began to feel more confident to venture, perhaps, outside the realm of romantic fiction, with the patient guidance of someone who understood. The heady scent of lily of the valley came up from the flower bed. As a single petal of honeysuckle fell upon her cheek, he lifted a tender finger to brush it away. Time stood still – at least for an hour or two. And by the time the sunset had painted the sky with its pastel ribbons Kate realised that, at long last she had found her Mr Darcy - the man who fell in love with the woman who read romantic fiction.

Her Father's Daughter

Her Father's Daughter

As she turned the key in the door Margaret had to stop herself from shouting "It's only me, Mam". It seemed so strange to find the house so quiet. She looked around the room. The table, with its green velvet cloth, looked empty without the china cup and saucer, all ready for the morning cup of tea and slice of cake. Mam was always old fashioned – no tea bags for her, only "real" tea would do. Through the open kitchen door she could see the tiny teapot and the tea strainer on the work surface. "One for each person and one for the pot!" she would call. "And remember to warm the pot first!" Margaret stretched out her hand to stroke the chair back and felt the delicate lace between her fingers. They were a golden wedding present from Aunty Ann. Now, both of them had gone, bless them. Only Aunty Meg was left, and she, poor thing, was at a complete loss without her sisters. Her gaze rested on the dusty television in the corner. Mam had hardly watched it since she had begun to lose her sight.

There wasn't much in the room, to be honest. A table, a chair, the television, and the settee which hid the old treadle organ that used to live in the parlour. The parlour had been a bedroom for Mam for the last four years as she became too infirm to use the stairs safely. Oh, the trouble they had trying to persuade her to move downstairs! "People will think I'm getting old!" she complained. "Well Mam" her brother sighed impatiently, "given that you are ninety three I think they might be right there!" But after she fell and broke her hip there was no other choice. And then the problem they had moving the organ! It weighed a ton. Huw, her brother, wanted to get rid of the old thing but Mam put her foot down, "That was your father's organ. If you are going to throw the organ out you may as well turn me out on the street at the same time. " "But Mam, you don't play it. Half the keys stick and there's a huge hole in the bellows. It's falling apart!" puffed Huw, his back against the side of the organ which was as stubborn as their mother when it came to moving. Memories flooded back. The gentle pleasure of listening to Dad practising ready for Sunday – and Mam singing along with the hymns in her shaking soprano voice. What would happen to the old organ now? Perhaps she should have a word with the local museum....

Her Father's Daughter

The door to the parlour swung open at her touch. The single bed looked so small, with its heavy candlewick bedspread and old fashioned quilted eiderdown. Who on earth would want a second hand bed, she wondered? The old oak wardrobe still stood in the corner. She opened the door and the smell of lavender "to keep the old moths away" hit her. Mam's clothes were still hanging there, apart from the ones she was wearing when she went into hospital. Margaret would need to sort them out – give them to Barnardos or something. She guessed that the chest of drawers would probably be full too.

She opened the first drawer. Her eye was taken by an old photograph album, its cover faded by the years and the corners tattered. She flicked through them – black and white pictures, some of them dating back to the 19th century. Mam with her brother in his black suit and her sisters all looking very serious in their white aprons, each child looked like a mini version of an adult. Gran, with her grey hair pulled into a tight bun – every hair scraped away from her forehead. How old would she have been then, she wondered? Forty? Less perhaps? She looked at least seventy. There was no sign of her Grandfather in the photo – he had been killed in the last days of the First World War. What must it have been like for Gran, raising seven children without her husband? She wondered what effect this had on her – and on the children. Mam was six years old then. Mam, Uncle John, Aunty Meg, Aunty Ann were still at school. Uncle Will was working as a gardener in the big house where Aunty Blod (named after Gran saw a performance of Joseph Parry's opera, so they said) worked as a kitchen maid. Uncle Harry was a baby. He died the following year from scarlet fever. Her fingers gently stroked the picture. A world long since vanished. Certainly, the family had seen their share of sadness. She decided to take the album to Aunty Meg in the rest home. She would be in her element talking about the days gone by.

On top of the chest of drawers was a photograph of her mother and father with Margaret's elder sister, Elisabeth – just before dad had gone off to war. Dad was in his military uniform. Elisabeth would have been less than a year old when he was called up to fight. She had often told Margaret that she had only the vaguest of memories of that time. She recalled Dad coming home – he must have been on leave – but Elisabeth didn't know him. This was not very surprising as he was away for a long time – at one point they had been told that he had been killed. Then they found out he was in a prisoner of war camp. Also on top of the chest was a photo of Dad with Elisabeth and Margaret on his lap with Mam standing behind cradling Huw in her arms. It had been taken on the beach at Porthcawl. Happy memories.

Margaret came back to herself. She would never finish sorting things out if she was going to sit down and look at everything. "This won't buy the baby a new frock nor mend the old one" she chided herself. She would look at the photos later with her sister. Huw wouldn't be interested – sentimental nonsense he would call it! Now what else was in the drawer? Seemingly endless lavender bags, enough handkerchiefs to open a shop and a small carved wooden box which looked very old. She opened it. It was full of old papers – Mam and Dad's wedding certificate June 1938; Elisabeth's birth certificate just under a year later and the telegram that arrived on the 12th of June 1940.

```
MRS  E  EVANS  17  STATION  ST  MERTHYR
TYDFIL  REGRET  TO  REPORT  YOUR  HUSBAND
EDWIN  ALBERT  C/JW  146443  IS  MISSING
PRESUMED  KILLED  ON  WAR  SERVICE  –
LETTER  FOLLOWS  –  COMMODORE  ROYAL  NAVY
BARRACKS  CHTAHAN.
```

Her Father's Daughter

So stark were those words. A further letter explained that her father's ship had been sunk and the majority of the crew lost. How must her mother have felt, thinking her husband to be dead, and with a daughter of less than two years of age to bring up? Margaret couldn't imagine how she would have coped.

Next she found a letter of sympathy from King George sent from Buckingham Palace.

```
        The Queen and I offer you
our   heartfelt   sympathy   in   your
great sorrow.
        We pray that your country's
gratitude  for  a  life  so  nobly
given in its Service may bring you
some measure of consolation
        George R.I.
```

Margaret didn't think that the king's words, no matter how kind and well-intended they were, would have helped much. She stared at the small bundle of letters from her father. It didn't feel right to look at them somehow. What else was there? Her own birth certificate - August 14th 1945; her brother's December 2nd 1947. She sat back. She wondered for how long her father had been missing?

There was another letter in faded blue ink.

18/12/1940

Dear Betty,

      I am sorry that it has taken me so long to reply to your letter, only this week did it reach me as a consequence of me being moved from one hospital to another. Thank you for your good wishes – I am recovering slowly and the nurses and doctors here have been golden to me. They say I may be walking soon.

      The last time that I saw Eddie he was in a small boat just before the ship went down. I was saved by one of our ships but I had thought that he had been pulled out by a French ship which was close by. I am so very sorry to hear your sad news.

      I would like to call on you when I am discharged from here if that would be agreeable to you. We can speak more then.

Warm regards

Tommy

Her Father's Daughter

Tommy who? It didn't say. He must have been one of Dad's friends.

At the bottom of the box was a small brown envelope addressed to her mother. The paper almost crumbled as she opened it to find a faded cheap quality paper note book. With trembling hands she persuaded herself to open her father's diary. It was written in pencil and in Welsh. She began to translate it....

June 2nd 1940

Our ship went down about a mile from the French coast. God only knows how many lost their lives. I was lucky to be picked up by a French fishing boat. I fell into the hands of a crew from Brittany. Well, there was a fine how do you do! I didn't speak a word of French and them no word of English but their tongue was close enough to the Welsh for us to understand each other. I have lost everything – my clothes were in rags and even my dog tag had gone down under the waves. The Frenchmen were very kind to me, and gave me food and clothing, although they did not have much to spare themselves.

Margaret didn't think she could bear to read any more of the detail of this, so she flicked forward to the next page.

June 4th 1940

I joined in with a group of resistance fighters from the same area and we made our way towards Paris, with me trying to find some British forces. I had no luck but heard there could be troops further up the coast who might be able to help.

A few pages on she found her father's description of the invasion of Paris.

June 15th 1940

We left Paris the same day that the Jerries arrived. Now that was something of a feat, I must tell you. We spent a whole week trying to get out of the city and it was a sight harder than getting in! For one thing, the railway was blocked so it was impossible to get a train. The bull had been through the china shop in Paris. No one had a clue what was going on. There was nothing for it but to try to walk to the next safe town.

The Nazis were behind us and overhead there was the almost constant sound of bombs dropping. Every time we got to a little village it had been flattened and they had left nothing. There was not a morsel of food left.

It all sounded desperate. She searched the diary hoping for some glimmer of hope, but instead she found..

July 1940

Oh my dearest Betty. It is my fervent hope that you have learnt that I am now in a Prisoner of War Camp - Stalag XIII-C in Hammelburg. I was captured with a group of French men from Brittany – I am still billeted with them at present. The Germans do not know that I am a Welshman. Food scarce. No contact with Red Cross yet.

August 1940

Oh Betty, my love, how I miss you and our little baby. I hope that this dreadful war will be over soon and we three will be walking hand in hand along the beach at Porthcawl as we two have done so many times.

September 1940

The authorities here think I am a Frenchman, so I dare not write to my family directly in case they think I am a spy. If they thought that they would have no hesitation in shooting me.

I am praying that my friends are safe and that they don't think I went down with the ship.

November 1940

The Red Cross have been allowed access to us. I hope to try to get a message to my family. "

The rest was too faint to be legible. Margaret found it very difficult to think of her father writing that diary. He was a real family man, always taking every opportunity to spend time with his daughters and son. And how much more difficult must it have been for her mother, back in Wales not knowing that her husband still lived and with a little girl to take care of? For how long, she wondered, did her mother think he was dead? Next to the diary was a letter from the Red Cross saying that her father was a prisoner of war. She studied the envelope. The post mark was faint and difficult to decipher. She remembered that her mother kept a magnifying glass at the side of her chair. She took the envelope back into the living room. With the aid of the glass she managed to read the date, March 20th 1945. Dad must have been home before Mam received that letter. What a shock that must have been. She went back to the box of papers.

People say, sometimes that the middle child is always awkward, lacking the confidence of the elder child and not as spoilt as the youngest. Perhaps that was why her father had always made more of a fuss of Margaret than his other two children. Her brother would be forever complaining that she was Daddy's favourite. It was a standing joke in the family that the reason Margaret had married late in life, too late for children of her own, was that she couldn't find a man who measured up to her father. There was some truth in that. She was the apple of his eye. The two of them were so similar; they had the same sense of humour and the same love of music. She was the only child who wanted to learn to play the organ. She smiled as she remembered his huge hands guiding her tiny fingers over the keys as she sat on three cushions to reach!

Next, she found the telegram saying that her father was on his way home. With a lump in her throat she imagined her mother's feelings. Years of thinking he was dead and suddenly hearing, first that he was still alive and then that he was coming home. She looked at the telegram again. And again. Something was not right here. Some mistake had been made. The telegram was dated May 1945. Three months before she, Margaret, was born.

She sat at the foot of the bed. She had heard of people being registered with the wrong date before. At one time the registrar only visited once a quarter – perhaps she wasn't born in August at all. Perhaps she was a winter baby.

She counted on her fingers, May, June, July, August, September, October, November, December. Was she born prematurely? Mam had never mentioned it. The more she thought about it she realised that her parents hadn't told her anything about her birth. A tide of emotions rushed through her head. She stared again at the photo of the family on Porthcawl beach, the three children were alike – their mother's curly hair and snub nose. But Elisabeth and Huw had blue eyes like both parents, whilst Margaret's were brown. Had she been adopted? Aunty Meg had no children. Had she had a child born the wrong side of the blanket whilst she was working as a maid, and then Mam and Dad had brought her up as their own? Was that why she, Margaret, had been named after her? She looked again at her birth certificate. She had been registered by her father. Father's name: Edwin Albert Williams - miner. Mother's name: Elisabeth May Williams - spouse.

There was nothing for it but to go to the Residential Home and talk to Aunty Meg. Perhaps there was a simple explanation. Perhaps Dad had been home for months when the letter arrived. Perhaps there was someone else called

Edward Albert Williams and the whole thing was a mistake. Perhaps......

As she walked to her car the weather seemed to echo her increasingly muddled thoughts. It was raining - that fine drizzle that falls like fog and soaks you to the skin. She arrived at the home and rang the bell. A disembodied voice replied from a speaker on the wall.

"Hello"

Margaret stepped closer to the white box.

"Hello, it's Margaret Williams. Margaret Thomas' niece. I've come to see my aunt."

The door opened. In the tiny porch she signed her name in the visitor's book and rubbed antibacterial gel on her hands. A short woman in a blue uniform came to open the internal door.

"How's it going? Mrs Thomas is in the lounge."

Margaret nodded.

"How is she keeping?"

"Pretty good. She'll be pleased to see you. Losing your mother was a big blow to her."

Her Father's Daughter

The place smelled of old people. Although everything was clean and the magnolia walls shone, the stench of pine disinfectant mingled with boiled cabbage hung in the air. She went down the narrow corridor along the green carpet to the lounge. The television was on. Loudly. Six people were sitting in arm chairs around the lounge. An old man was watching a strangely orange man selling antiques on the screen. Irony there, perhaps. Another man was staring blankly out of the window. Two elderly ladies were sleeping. Aunty Meg was trying to have a conversation with the woman sitting next to her – without much success to be honest. The woman couldn't hear her. The two looked at the doorway to see who had come in. Her aunt smiled broadly.

"Maggie, love! There's lovely to see you!"

She turned to her neighbour and shouted "Here's my niece, Margaret. My sister Betty's girl. You remember my sister Betty?"

The woman searched Margaret's face with tired eyes. Then she smiled.

"Hello Betty. Haven't seen you since a long time."

Aunty Meg sighed and shook her head.

"In a world of her own, she is."

Margaret felt sorry for her aunt. Although she was physically fragile her mind was still sharp. How did she cope there, she wondered. Her niece felt guilty for not visiting her more regularly. She pulled a chair closer to her.

"I was clearing Mam's things – I found this photograph album. I thought you might like to see the photos."

Tears filled the old woman's eyes. Although it had been more than a month the wound of loss was still young. She opened the book. A photo of Mam, Aunty Meg and Aunty Ann in their best frocks and huge hats. The date was written in ink in the corner "May 16 1928 – Will and Mary's wedding".

Aunty Meg smiled.

"Look. Don't we all look so young? Your Mam was only 16. Will in his black suit! Look at him holding his bowler hat with his finger and thumb and his white gloves over his hand! And Mary in her long gown and cap with a veil down to her waist. Height of fashion it was at the time! Fair play!" She began to laugh. "Oh dearie me!"

Mam and Dad's wedding was next. Dad in his suit and collar which looked as if it was half strangling him. Mam with her hand on his arm, an enormous bouquet covering half of her white dress. She was wearing a hat reminiscent of "The Queen of Hearts" in Disney's version of "Alice in Wonderland" with a long veil at the back which went down to her calves. They were smiling happily. It was hard to believe that the war would be coming only a year later.

"Aunty Meg...." Margaret wasn't sure how she was going to begin this.

"Yes, love?"

"There were lots of other things in the drawer. Things from the war time."

The old lady's eyes scrutinised her. Did she know what Margaret was going to say?

"Why don't we go back to my room to talk, is it? Hard to converse with anybody with that old television shouting away..."

Margaret pushed her aunt's wheelchair towards her room. Silence. Were they both afraid to speak? The room was sparsely furnished. An armchair stood next to the single bed, opposite a small TV on the wall, a wardrobe, a window. Almost like a prison cell. Aunty Meg sat down heavily in the armchair. Margaret went out to get a hard plastic chair from the corridor.

"Now then…" the old woman's head was shaking.

"There was a telegram saying that Dad had died…"

"Yes, there was. Your mother broke her heart. We all thought she would never get over it."

"But she did…."

"Yes. In time."

"When did she find out that he was still alive?"

"When the letter arrived from the Red Cross"

"That was in 1945…. "

Her aunt nodded.

"Five years. Your poor mother thought your father was had been killed for nearly five years."

Margaret sat in silence trying to take the words in. Five years. From June 1940 until…. She had to find out.

"When did he come home?"

"After the allies liberated the prisoner of war camps just before the end of the war."

Margaret looked at her.

"Was I adopted?"

"No of course not. Why would you think that, and you and your Mam so alike..?."

"Aunty Meg, I was born three months after my father came home from the war. What happened? Was Mam unfaithful?"

"Of course she wasn't! Your mother would never do that. You should know better....."

"Was she ....?" She couldn't say the words out loud, thinking of her mother.

"No. No. Nothing like that. She remarried."

"Remarried? How? Who?"

"Does it matter? It is all so long ago, she thought your Dad had been killed. When she found out he was alive, it was Eddie she chose."

Margaret's head was spinning. Her beloved father, the apple of her eye ... he wasn't her father. Her world had been turned on its head.

"Who....was.... my ...." She couldn't even say the word "Father".

"Tommy, a friend of your father's. He wrote to your mother while he was in hospital – he lost his leg. Then he came to see her.... he had a job in the bank where he could sit down. You've got to remember, love – your mother and I were brought up without a father after our father was killed in the Great War. She knew well enough was it was like to raise children without a man around. Tommy was lonely and he thought the world of your mother. In the end they got married. But when the news came about Eddie the two of them knew what had to be done. The marriage was annulled. No one could ever take your father's place in her heart."

"So, Tommy is ..."

Aunty Meg gave her a stern look. Then she rose in her seat to get closer to her.

"Now then, my girl......Who was there for you all through your life?" her voice was no more than a whisper. "Who looked after you when you were ill? And whose signature is on your birth certificate?"

"Daddy" came the tearful reply.

Aunty Meg was right. It didn't matter who her biological father was. There was much more than genes to being a parent. She thought of her mother. She had lost her father in the First World War and had lived in poverty as a result. Of course she didn't want the same thing for Elisabeth. Of course she would have married Dad's friend — her last connection with him. And Dad? He worshipped Mam. He was a kind man, generous to a fault. He would have understood.

"What happened to him?"

"Tommy? He went to live in Canada."

As far away as possible. Margaret could understand that.

"Did he come back?"

"Once – for his mother's funeral. With his wife."

A half-forgotten memory came back to her of a man coming to the house, walking with a cane. Mam had introduced her to him and said he was going home to Canada the next morning. She remembered him staring at her for a long time without saying a word. And she wondered why.....

"He died years ago. Your parents had a card to say."

There was nothing more to say then. Aunty Meg caught hold of her niece's sleeve.

"Let the dead bury the dead, love. Your dad loved you. He was a good father to you."

She nodded. He was. He was a perfect father. It would not have been possible to have a better one. She was the apple of his eye. She adored him too.

She stood up to go.

"Thank you Aunty Meg. I don't think I'll mention this to Elisabeth and Huw."

"No, there's no point, is there?"

"No. Dad was my father."

She was almost at the door when a question came into her head.

"Did he have any children?"

"Yes. A son and a daughter I think."

"Do they know?"

"I don't know, love."

She closed her eyes. The old lady's head was nodding. Margaret left the photographs with her aunt and gently kissed her furrowed forehead. She was half asleep. Margaret closed the door and walked out into the fresh air.

Tommy was dead - there would be no chance to ask him how he felt about leaving his child. Did he ever think of her? And so, she had a half brother and sister somewhere in Canada. Did they know about her? If they did they hadn't got in contact. Did they have families? Perhaps she had half nieces and nephews. All in their secure happy world - as she had been that morning. Did she have the right to turn their worlds upside down by telling them? Suddenly she knew the answer. No, she decided. She lifted her head and walked

Her Father's Daughter

towards her car. After all, she was her father's daughter – that's what everyone always said. It was all in the past – and sometimes that is where the past is meant to be kept.

Marvelous Mrs Rushmore

Marvelous Mrs Rushmore

Sometimes Sally wondered how her two children could be so different. Her older daughter, Emma, had found school easy. She shone, was always the one who was chosen to read in assembly, always had "A"s on her report and her teachers enthused about her abilities. It was clear she was going to go far. But for Tommy it had always been a struggle. He battled with reading and writing. Maths had made him cry. It had got to the point where he didn't want to go to school at all. They had talked to the head teacher about it, who had set in motion the process of having Tommy tested for learning difficulties as they thought he might be dyslexic. The tests came back but didn't really help. He had "non-specific learning difficulties" which didn't require an educational statement or qualify for any extra help. His parents despaired. But all that changed when he went into Mrs Rushmore's class.

Suddenly Tommy seemed to find himself. It was as if someone had given him the key to a door which had previously been locked to him. He began to flourish. He came home from school excited to talk about the day's events. He always seemed to have something new to tell his parents these days. Last week it was a new way of remembering how to spell the word "friend" -"There's an "I" in it – "I" have to be the one to make a friend"; the week before it had been a rule about plurals "Did you know if a word ends in "S" you put an "es" on the end? Kisses, glasses, rugby passes!". Sally and her husband Geoff had been relieved and overjoyed.

Tommy was now sitting at the dining table, waving a bacon sandwich in the air with one hand and gesticulating with the other.

"Today we learnt the tricks for the nine times table. It's really easy. I think it's my favourite now. Can you do it Mum?"

Maths had never been his mother's strong point. She thought about it.

"Let's see... One nine is nine, two nines are eighteen, three nines are... Let me work it out, eighteen plus nine is...."

"No, Mum, you're doing it all wrong – making it hard for yourself!" Tommy was almost bursting waiting to tell her.

"Well go on then, clever clogs!" It was wonderful to see him like this.

"First you take one away from the number you want to multiply with. So "one" take away "one" is zero. Zero nine. One nine is nine. Then put the number you want to multiply with one taken away in front and take away one – two – one – in front of nine - two nines are eighteen, three nines are twenty seven, four nines are thirty six, five nines are forty five, six nines are fifty four, seven nines are sixty three, eight nines are seventy two, ten nines are ninety, eleven nines are ninety nine, twelve nines are one hundred and eight. It's a pattern – see?"

"Well done! That's very clever. "His mother was very pleased.

"But that's not all! There's another way of checking that you've got it right. Did you know that all the numbers in the nine times table add up to nine?"

"Do they?" his mother had never heard of that one.

"Yes. Nine, then one and eight are nine, two and seven are nine, three and six are nine – it even works after a hundred. Thirteen nines are one hundred and seventeen – one – one and seven makes nine!"

"Well, I am impressed! And who told you that, then?"

"Mrs Rushmore. Maths is easy when you can see the patterns, Mum. And English – there are just rules – and when you know the rules it's easy. I love school!"

What a transformation! Sally brushed away a tear. She was looking forward to meeting the marvellous Mrs Rushmore. She seemed to be the Mary Poppins of teachers. All of the parents at the school gate had said how much their children liked her – and whatever it was that she was doing, it certainly seemed to be working for Tommy. His self-confidence had improved more than they had ever thought possible. Before, he never wanted to bring friends home to play but now he seemed to have a wide circle of friends and there was almost always someone coming for tea every week. His best friend was a quiet boy called "Matthew" who had moved into the area that school year. Matthew's mum was disabled so sometimes Sally collected them both from the school gate and then his father would collect him on his way home from work. The little boy didn't talk much about his mother's disability, although some days he would say things like "Mummy was hurting a lot today so I helped her with breakfast". It seemed rude to inquire further. He was a very polite little boy, and always well turned out. Sally hadn't met his mother, as it was his dad who took him to school and his grandmother who usually collected him.

"Rebecca isn't very good in the mornings" his father had told her. "She would love to collect him from school but it is too cold for her yet. When the weather warms up a bit we'll see."

"Well, Tommy Phillips" said his mother as she cleared away the tea things "we shall see what Mrs Rushmore has to say about you tomorrow night at parent's evening"

Tommy nodded. "I got a silver star for my reading today. And I've got another new reading book."

"That's very good. Now you go and watch the children's programmes on the television while I clear up and then we'll have a look at this new reading book."

The boy bolted from the table. His sister rolled her eyes.

"He'll be watching the cartoons again. I'll go upstairs to do my homework."

Sally nodded. "Good girl. You can come down and watch what you want to while I'm listening to him read."

As she washed the dishes she smiled to herself. Life was good and it seemed that the worries of the past had been left behind. Like all families, they had their challenges but on the whole she was very content.

The next afternoon Sally waited with the other parents to see the teacher. Her appointment was for 4:15 so she looked around the classroom at the children's work as she waited. Matthew's father was sitting at a table with his wife and the teacher. Sally tried not to stare at the woman in the wheelchair. Meeting people with disabilities was always awkward, she felt. What exactly was the protocol? Should you ask what the problem was or just ignore it? Was it rude to ask? She recalled a meeting with a doctor who's right arm was truncated. She hadn't known what to do. She shook his left hand, which felt odd, but her husband had shaken the truncated arm. Which was right? She didn't know. There weren't any children with disabilities in her school. The para-olympics had been brilliant – who knew people like that could achieve so much – but of course those people were exceptional she reasoned. It was so difficult to deal with ordinary people with disabilities.

She cast an eye at the other lady at the table. So this was the marvellous Mrs Rushmore. Strange, she didn't look as Sally had imagined her. Not like Mary Poppins at all. She was about the same age as Sally, with a tight lipped mouth. She certainly didn't look like the energetic woman Tommy described – in fact she looked quite tired and drawn. Perhaps it was true about how hard junior school teachers worked.

Matthew's father looked very happy as he thanked Mrs Rushmore for all she was doing for his son. He moved away from the table and the teacher went with him. Perhaps there was something else she had to show him. Sally chided herself for being so nosey. Then the woman in the wheelchair called "Mrs Phillips?" Ah, she probably wanted to thank her for looking after Matthew. Sally went over to the table and sat down. Matthew's mother was a sweet looking lady with a broad smile. She put out her hand to shake Sally's.

"Tommy is such an enthusiastic boy. He's coming on in leaps and bounds" she said.

Sally blushed with pride. Matthew must have told her all about him.

"Yes, we did have a few worries about him, but since he has been in this class there seems to be no stopping him."

The other woman laughed. "That's very kind of you but I can assure you it is all down to his hard work. Now, I have his books here. Shall we start with his Maths? He really does have a flair for the subject…."

Sally checked herself. Was this Mrs Rushmore? But it couldn't be! The Mrs Rushmore Tommy had described was full of life and always had a funny story to tell them. This woman was in a wheelchair. She couldn't be Mrs Rushmore! Perhaps she was a teaching assistant. Tommy had said they had a teaching assistant who helped Mrs Rushmore. But he hadn't said she was in a wheelchair.

She began to look at the maths book. Tommy did seem to be doing well – there were a lot of ticks and stars – only the occasional cross – and where there was she could see he had done correction and got it right almost all of the time. This was certainly very much better than she could have hoped for. But who was she talking to? She needed to find a delicate way to ask.

"Tommy said there was a teaching assistant in the class"

The woman smiled. "Yes, Miss Thomas. She helps with some of the group activities and some of the things that are difficult for me physically. She isn't here tonight. Did you wish to speak to her?"

Sally didn't know where to put herself. How embarrassing! They talked about Tommy's progress in other subjects and also about his friendship with Matthew.

"They seem to have really clicked. They are both nice boys."

When she got home she congratulated Tommy on his excellent progress and then couldn't help herself saying

"You never mentioned that Mrs Rushmore was in a wheelchair."

Tommy looked at her as if she had just made the silliest comment ever.

Marvelous Mrs Rushmore

"What difference does that make? I didn't think it was important." His eyes were wide. Sally struggled to explain.

"It's just unusual. She is a very good teacher though."

"She's the best" grinned her son. "It makes me try all the harder because she tries really hard."

Suddenly she could see why Mrs Rushmore was so inspirational. Not only was she a brilliant teacher, but seeing her overcome her disability, must have a positive effect on the children who were struggling to overcome their own difficulties.

She said as much to Matthew's father when he called to collect him the following week.

"Yes" he agreed. "Matthew is much more settled here. He doesn't feel that he has to be ashamed of his mother's condition as his teacher is disabled too. There are times when my wife needs to use a wheelchair – before he was in this class Matthew didn't want to go out with her then as the other children made fun of his mother. Now none of his friends comment. It has helped us all."

Walking up to the school gate Sally reflected on the many things she took for granted – her health, her family – just being able to do things! Her son might never be as academically bright as her daughter, but she felt that whatever he did he would now achieve his potential. Thanks to the Marvelous Mrs Rushmore.

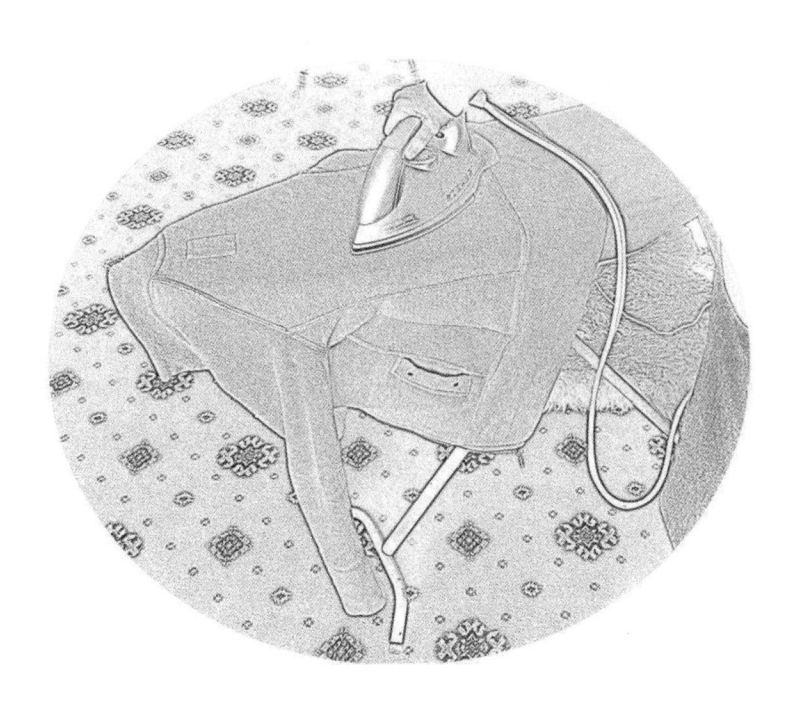

The Ironing Lady

The Ironing Lady

Mari had always hated ironing. She gazed with a sinking heart at the huge heap of clothes before her, feeling rather like the unfortunate girl in the story of Rumpelstilskin. But this time there would be no magical fairy to do all the work. "Ah well", she thought to herself, "better make a start". Although, perhaps she would have a cup of something before she started – after all ironing always made her thirsty. Yes, a cuppa and a chocolate biscuit. Well, it would be at least two hours, at least, before the first client came to collect it.....

She lifted the iron from the cupboard and pulled out the plastic container which held the water. With the television to keep her company she decided to sort the clothes first; garments which needed a cool iron first and things that needed a hot iron last. She had learned this lesson the hard way after scorching Mrs Morgan-Jenkins' silk blouse. There was no way that Mari would ever be able to afford to buy such grand clothes as those of Mrs Morgan-Jenkins, National Opera. Silk blouses, linen trousers – everything that was awkward to iron! Mari wasn't too

The Ironing Lady

bothered about that – it was the way the woman spoke to her that was the problem –as if she was a five year old child. She always seemed to be in a bad mood and Mari was the one she lashed out at. Mari wasn't stupid, as Mrs Morgan-Jenkins always seemed to infer. She had a good degree in Journalism – but by the time she had left university there were no jobs available. The local newspaper closed, other papers were making hundreds of people redundant. At first she had tried for pretty much every job that came up at the job centre or in the paper, but every time she was told that she was over qualified, or too young, or too old, or that she didn't have enough experience. She decided to start her own business. But what could she do that wouldn't cost a fortune to set up? Her debts from getting her degree meant that she wasn't likely to get a loan, and she didn't really like the idea of going into further debt. She looked around her and thought about her practical skills. She wanted to write stories, and still did so in her spare time, but that wasn't going to earn her any money in the short term at least. Almost everything required a big investment. So, she settled on starting "Pressed For Time Ironing Service". She already had a decent steam iron and an ironing board. She put an advertisement in the local supermarket and the work began to come in. She had just over a dozen customers which gave her an income of about £200 a week – much better than the dole.

But, oh, it was boring work! Whilst she ironed she thought about the lives of the people who owned the clothes. Mrs Morgan-Jenkins, who sang in the chorus of the National Opera, whilst her husband played the violin in the orchestra – expensive designer clothes – Mari imagined their life – parties, eating out, holidays in the sun overseas..... Another world!

She didn't mind so much ironing clothes for Mrs Jones, her former junior school teacher. She was a lady who always smiled a lot, even though arthritis had bent her body and knotted her hands into deformed shapes. She was always grateful to Mari and praised her work. Mari felt sad that such a kind woman had suffered so much.

She finished the clothes for Mrs Jones, filled the tank on the iron and started on Mrs Morgan-Jenkins' blouses. She lifted a pink silk shirt from the heap in the clothes basket. The heady scent of expensive perfume wafted up at her. No matter how many times they were washed Mrs Morgan-Jenkins' clothes always carried her signature fragrance. As she was placing the garment on the ironing board she noticed there was a lump in the pocket. "I had better take that out straight away, in case ink goes over everything and gives Madam another excuse to tell me off" she said to herself. She pulled out the wrinkled piece of paper from the pocket. Something important perhaps? As she smoothed out the creases with her fingers she recognized it at once. A lottery ticket.

She used the cool iron to get the piece of paper flat again. It was quite tattered but the numbers were clear. There had been something on the local news last night about the lottery. Someone local had won thirteen million pounds but no one had claimed the prize yet. Could it be....?

No, it was a daft idea. What would be the chances, anyway? There was no point in looking. She carried on with her work, but the lottery ticket was winking at her from the table and preying on her mind. Someone had to win, she supposed. Finally she pressed the red button on the television remote control to look at the lottery numbers.

The Ironing Lady

1   13   19   21   27   29

She looked at the ticket.

1   13   19   21   27   29

She looked again. This couldn't be possible. It must be for a different date. She checked. Twice. Then she sat down.

In her hand was the winning ticket – a ticket worth thirteen million pounds.

What was she to do? It wasn't her ticket... but then again... if she hadn't pulled it out of the pocket and ironed it flat no one would be able to claim the prize anyway. She began to imagine how her world would change if she had a thirteen million pounds. She would buy a house, go on holiday, and pay off the mortgage for her parents! With that much money anything was possible. She could even start up a new local newspaper – or a magazine for women.....

But it wasn't her ticket. She would have to tell Mrs. Morgan-Jenkins. But.... they didn't *need* the money – they had plenty. Mari could do a lot more good with the money than they would she was sure.

In an impulse she picked up the phone and dialed the number on the back of the ticket. A disembodied voice asked for the numbers on the ticket. Trembling she read them out and the code on the ticket. There was a pause, and then the voice asked for her name. Mari put the phone down quickly shaking from head to toe. What was she going to do?

She heard the sound of a car pulling up outside and the clip clop of Mrs Morgan-Jenkins' designer high heels walking towards her front door. The doorbell rang. Mari still had the ticket in her hand. She opened the door.

"I'm a little early. Is it ready?" enquired Mrs Morgan–Jenkins frostily.

"Almost. Just one shirt to go. Would you like to wait?"

"I suppose so. No sense in making an extra journey."

Mari's conscience got the better of her.

"I found this in the pocket of one of your blouses. I've done my best to make it legible."

The Ironing Lady

She handed over the crumpled ticket. Mrs Morgan-Jenkins looked embarrassed.

"Thank you. One always likes to support good causes."

Mari finished ironing the shirt, put it on the hanger and put a clear plastic bag over the shirts and blouses.

"There you are."

"Thank you. How much do I owe you?"

"Fifteen pounds please."

Mrs Morgan-Jenkins opened her purse.

"Do you have change? I only have a twenty pound note."

"Yes. Here we are…" Mari took a five pound note from her purse on the table. "I'll just get your receipt."

She wrote out a receipt in her book, checking that the carbon copy had come out properly.

"Have to keep the taxman happy."

"I'm glad to see that someone keeps proper records. You hear of so many people fiddling their books these days."

Mari nodded. Should she say anything? It was up to Mrs Morgan-Jenkins to check the numbers. What if she didn't? The money would go to a good cause – that wouldn't be so bad. But – Mari would always know ... Oh blow it – she had to tell her.

"Mrs Morgan-Jenkins...."

"What is it? I'm in a bit of a hurry...."

"The ticket..."

"Ticket?"

"The lottery ticket."

"What about it? Surely you're not expecting me to share any winnings with you just because you took it out of the pocket?"

Mari decided not to answer that one.

"The numbers were on the television earlier. I think you may have won."

Mrs Morgan-Jenkins looked at her as if she had just announced that she had conclusive proof that the moon was, indeed, made of green cheese.

The Ironing Lady

"I'm sure I haven't."

"I'm sure you have. Look." Mari switched on the television, pressed the red button and called up the lottery numbers.

Mrs Morgan-Jenkins looked at the numbers, and then she looked at the ticket. Then she looked at the numbers again. She sat down and her mouth opened and closed silently like a goldfish.

"Mrs Morgan-Jenkins…. Are you alright? Would you like me to get you a glass of water?"

Mrs Morgan-Jenkins nodded. Mari brought her the drink. She sipped it slowly.

"Would you just check it again for me?" she handed the ticket back to Mari. Mari couldn't let on that she had already checked it twice.

"It's correct. Congratulations."

What more could she say? Mrs Morgan-Jenkins gathered herself together, picked up the ironing and got into her car without saying another word.

The Ironing Lady

Well that was that. Mari's chance of a fortune had gone. Although she felt that she had done the right thing she was half kicking herself for being so honest.

She got on with the rest of her work, put away the iron and the ironing board, did her accounts for the day and then switched on the news. The news reader was looking very pleased with herself.

"The National Lottery has confirmed that a Welsh woman was one of the six winners in this week's Lotto draw. The woman is from the South Wales Valleys but wishes to remain anonymous. The six winners will each collect thirteen million four thousand three hundred and twenty seven pounds each. The winner is said to be delighted. Well, it wasn't me. If that wasn't you either, let's see if Derek can cheer us up with the weather forecast."

Mari felt quite flat. So that was that then.

Mrs Morgan-Jenkins didn't bring any ironing the following week. Or the week after that. It was three weeks later when the doorbell rang and Mr and Mrs Morgan-Jenkins stood at the door. Mr Morgan-Jenkins had a large bouquet of flowers in his hand.

The Ironing Lady

"These are for you."

Mari didn't know what to say. She mumbled

"Thank you" and "Come in".

Mr Morgan-Jenkins handed her the flowers.

"We wanted to thank you personally for rescuing the lottery ticket."

Mari nodded. "All part of the service." She forced a smile.

"It will make our lives so much easier you see." Mrs Morgan-Jenkins explained. Would it really? Mari thought they had it easy enough as it was. Mr Morgan-Jenkins stood up.

"People think there isn't a lot to playing in the orchestra or singing in the chorus. They don't think about the long hours sacrificed practicing when you are a child – all the times you wanted to go and play with your friends but you couldn't because you had to practice. They don't realize how physically demanding it is – rehearsals by day and then performances by night."

"Not to mention watching what you eat, not drinking alcohol – never being able to accept social events because you are always working…." added Mrs Morgan-Jenkins.

"We enjoyed it for many years. I don't want to pretend that we didn't. But we are getting older now…" Mr Morgan-Jenkins shook his head.

"This money will give us enough to pay the mortgage and actually be able to LIVE". Mrs Morgan-Jenkins was smiling. At least that was what it looked like, although Mari half wondered if it could be wind.

"Anyway – our bags are packed, we're selling up and going off to live somewhere warmer."

"Yes, it has always been our dream" his wife added.

Then off they went – waving as they went.

Mari looked around her flat. She had worked so hard for everything in it. It had been years since she went on holiday. Ah well. It sounded as though their lives were not as glamorous as she had thought. Good luck to them. Everyone deserves a little luck.

The Ironing Lady

She picked up the bouquet and took it into the kitchen to arrange the flowers. She cut the cellophane and removed the envelope with her name on it which was stapled to it.

"I wonder what they have written on the card?" she mused, opening it. There was a small card with roses on the front. She opened it.

"To Mari – thank you for your honesty and integrity."

She opened the folded piece of paper inside it and then gasped...

The Ironing Lady

The next day Mari stood in the queue in the bank as she had so often done, to pay in her takings for the week so that she could pay her bills. Today, however there was more of a spring in her step as she handed the bundle of cheques over to the cashier. The girl swiped Mari's bank card and then began processing the cheques. Then she stopped and stared, looking first at the screen and then at Mari. Then she handed the slip over to Mari to sign, saying

"Would you like to see our investment manager?"

"Yes." Said Mari "I rather think I would."

The manager opened the door to his office, smiling broadly.

"Miss Ellis? Do come in. I must say, it isn't every day we get a millionairess in here. How can I help you?"

Status Change

Status Change

Cerys flew through the door as if her feet had wings. The broadest smile she had worn for a while was on her face. The date had gone really well – again. The third date. And of course, every one knew what that meant. She pulled off her coat and threw it vaguely at the hook on the back of the door, without looking to see if it had missed or not. And then she took her phone from her bag. She went straight to Facebook. There, in front of her was her own page:

Name: Cerys Thomas

City: Swansea

Single

Birthday: June 8

She held her breath – and wondered if Rhodri had got home yet.

She took a peek at his status.

Status Change

Name: Rhodri Lloyd

City: Swansea

Single

Birthday   December 2

She checked the time – a few minutes after midnight. He was still on his way she reasoned. Should she wait for a bit? Should she let him change his status first? No –Rhodri was lovely and he had said that he thought she was lovely too. He had actually said those words that very evening. And more...

"You are the girl of my dreams"

She sighed, remembering every little detail. The way the wind caught his hair, making it fall over one eye and the casual way he swept it back with his hand. The way he closed his eyes when they kissed. He was serious about her, she was sure. And, oh, he was so good looking!

Then she decided. She would make the first move. She changed her status from

Status Change

"Single" to *"In a relationship"*.

It was, of course, too early to tell the whole world who exactly she was in a relationship with – that would make her look too keen. A girl had to keep some self-respect.

She sat back on her chair. That was it. As soon as Rhodri saw her status he would know that she really liked him. It would be up to him, then, to make the next move. She wondered if he had got home yet.

She clicked the "Refresh" button.

Three people had "liked" her status change. Was Rhodri one of them? She just had to check.

Disappointment. Only her friends had "liked" her new status. But on the other hand they had commented.

Ffion: Sounds exciting babe. Who is the lucky boy then?

Meleri: That was quick. It's only been a week since you and Gwyn finished.

Cerys scowled. Meleri could be a right bitch at times.

Catrin: Oh, good for you. When will we meet him then?

She replied to each one.

@ Ffion – too early to tell you all that.

@ Catrin – we'll see.

@ Meleri – three weeks, not a week – although everything had been over for a couple of months after what he did!

She picked her coat up off the floor, put it on the hook and went into the kitchen to make a cuppa – and she fancied a chocolate biscuit to go with it.

She clicked "Refresh" again. One person had "liked" and there was one new comment. Rhodri?

No, disappointment again.

Lisa had "liked" but she hadn't left a comment. Jealousy, probably. She hadn't had a boyfriend for months. It was Meleri who had responded.

Status Change

If it's too early to say who he is then maybe you shouldn't be saying you are in a relationship. And if you hadn't been flirting with that tall bloke all evening my brother wouldn't have gone off with Siwan. They are still a couple, thought you might like to know.

Now Cerys flipped. If she hadn't have had three glasses of wine she would have thought twice before having a public slanging match on Facebook. Sometimes wine can steal both your conscience and your common sense.

Good luck to them. She must have no self-respect to put up with your brother. Still, it is early days, I guess – and she'll learn. I did!

She looked again at Rhodri's status. He hadn't changed it. He **must** have got home by now! It was a quarter to one now.

She finished her cuppa and had more than one chocolate digestive. She had an early lecture the next morning. To be honest, she should be in bed by now. But she wanted to see Rhodri's status change.

She went upstairs to clean her teeth and change into her pyjamas. She looked at her phone again. The Internet connection wasn't as good upstairs and it took an age. There were no new "likes" for her status but there was a new comment. She checked it.

Meleri: Gwyn says there must have been something wrong with him to go out with you in the first place. There must be something the matter with your new bloke as well. He'll learn too!

Furious, Cerys responded immediately

Yes – you're right – there is something wrong with your brother – a lot of things. Rhodri's more of a man than he'll ever be!

Wine can be such a dangerous thing sometimes.....

She looked at the clock again. It was quarter past one by now. Another glance at Rhodri's status. He still hadn't changed it. Perhaps he had gone straight to bed. He did say he had a nine o'clock lecture the next day. Or perhaps he hadn't got a good connection in his flat. Time for her to get to sleep too, or she would never be up in time for Peter

Status Change

Evans' lecture. She didn't mind too much missing an hour of someone else's lectures but Peter Evans always made some snide remark when someone was late. As he had done last week.

"Good Afternoon, Miss Thomas."

"Sorry – couldn't find the room."

"You'll have to use a map next time – or come with someone else who IS able to get here on time perhaps?"

"Sorry."

She had sat down knowing that everyone in the room was staring at her. She didn't want to be late for him again.

One more look. No one had responded. She closed her eyes and decided not to put her phone on "silent" just in case Rhodri rang.......

The alarm rang mercilessly. Eight o'clock. Her head was pounding and her stomach was doing somersaults. She was just about to hit the "snooze" button when three things came back into her mind.

Status Change

1. Firstly – she wondered if Rhodri had changed his status yet.
2. Secondly – she had had a public row on Facebook with Meleri – hope no one else had seen it.
3. Thirdly – Peter Evans was lecturing that morning so she couldn't be late for him again.

She looked at her phone – but the battery was flat. She had forgotten to plug it in to the charger last night. Wine makes you forgetful. She reached over the small bedside cabinet for the plug. Nothing for it but to wait for it to charge while she had a shower.

Under the shower she heard a "ping" from the phone. She rushed out of the bathroom with a towel wrapped around her, soap in her eyes, body dripping and leaving a trail of wet foot prints on the carpet. She pulled the phone from the plug but her eyes were stinging so much that she couldn't see who had sent the text message. She went back into the bathroom to rinse her hair. Once she could see clearly she went back to the phone. Disappointment. It wasn't Rhodri who had sent the text – it was Catrin.

Status Change

Can't believe you had a full on slanging match with Mel on FB. Everyone talking about it today. OOPS!

Cerys stood still and stared at the wall. She couldn't remember exactly what she had said. Something concerning Gwyn she thought.....Not so bad.... Then she remembered mentioning Rhodri too. Oh no! She just HAD to check his status – to see if they were "Official" or not. Everyone knows you don't give the name of your new boyfriend until both of you have changed your statuses on Facebook. She checked. No – Rhodri was still "SINGLE". Perhaps he hadn't seen it. She went to her own timeline to try to delete the conversation from last night. But her phone wouldn't let her delete it – she would have to use a proper computer. She turned to the clock again. There was just enough time for her to call into the Resource Centre before going to her lecture. She would have to go without breakfast to make it. Her stomach was churning after drinking too much the night before and to be honest she was starving. But there was no choice. So she dressed as quickly as she could and shot out through the door.

Status Change

Half way up the hill her legs gave way underneath her – she felt weak. She had to sit on the low wall outside one of the houses for a minute or two before carrying on. She was fighting to keep the contents of her stomach in place. With a sigh of relief she reached the doors of the Resource Centre – but the doors were locked. A piece of paper was fixed to the window.

THE RESOURCE CENTRE IS CLOSED DUE TO A POWER CUT.

What? How was she going to delete the conversation now?

She staggered down the steps towards the room where a crowd of people were waiting for Peter Evans. She felt so ill that she wasn't sure she could face it. They were joining with another Group for today – the Media Studies lot or something like that she thought. She made her way gingerly into the room, stumbled up the steps and half fell into a seat at the back where she hoped she could hide for the rest of the session without drawing further attention to herself. At least she wasn't late. The lecturer was speaking but Cerys wasn't listening. It was as if his voice was far, far away. She suddenly felt very hot and the room was spinning. Then, ever so slowly, she slid off the seat and landed on the carpet in an untidy heap. When she opened her eyes everyone was staring at her and the room was completely silent. She tried to lift her head but the effort was too much. Then, she saw something that should have sobered her up in a second. There in the opposite corner of the room a familiar face was looking at her intently. A guy from the group that was joining them that day. Rhodri!

Could things get any worse, she wondered?

He rushed over to her and she felt his strong arms lift her back into her seat. Someone was offering her water whilst Rhodri was telling her to put her head down. Slowly she began to feel a bit better. Rhodri asked for permission to take her to the nurse. She ambled out on shaking legs - like Bambi on ice.

She said nothing.

"Have you eaten today, Chick?"

Status Change

She shook her head.

"That's what's the matter, I'll bet. Better see the nurse and get checked out, yeah?"

"Sorry" she mumbled.

"For what, Chick?"

Didn't he know? She looked at him with eyes full of tears.

"Did you see Facebook this morning?"

"Facebook? No. Not at all. I've got an account but I never use it. I'd rather talk to people face to face. Why? What have I missed?"

"Errrrm – nothing.... it doesn't matter anyway..."

Then he smiled a huge, broad White smile at her.

"Oh, I get it. Were you waiting for me to change my status?"

Her eyes said everything but her lips said "No, not really... it's early days yet..."

"It is. But like I said last night, I think you're lovely. We'll see how things go, yeah?"

Status Change

She nodded. The nurse gave her something to rehydrate her system, and then on the way back she noticed that the Resource Centre was open now.

"Right, I feel better now but I can't face that lot. You go back to the lecture and let me know what I've missed will you? There's something I have to do…"

In front of the computer screen once more she deleted the conversation from the night before and then updated her status.

Single…..

But living in hope!

The Bardolino Suite

The Maitre D's Recommendation

The Maître D's Recommendation

Diana Jones stepped out of the doors of Verona airport, threw back her head and let the warmth of the Italian sunshine caress her skin. Two weeks of complete relaxation in her favourite hotel in her favourite place in her favourite country. She picked up her case and made her way to the coach, pausing to pass the time of day with the driver. She was happy for the opportunity to practice her Italian. How she relished her holidays here! She would go to Venice, walk along the canals, window shop and feed the birds in Saint Mark's square, taking in the human statues, the masked actors and the honeymoon couples gazing into each other's eyes in gondolas; she would go twice to the opera in Verona, La Bohème and Aida this year, sitting on the cushion she had brought with her while the music filled her head, the spectacle, the sounds, the scents drowning her senses; she would take in the sights of Firenze with every view bringing in yet more lovely buildings – but best of all she would walk by the lakeside to her beloved Bardolino past the prettily painted fishing boats, take her usual seat at the café and listen to the singing floating across the night air. Was there, she thought, any place on earth more lovely than Lake Garda? The snow-capped mountains at the north end, the view from the mountain cable car, the cows with their great bells slowly munching at the lush green grass, the wide water as blue as cornflowers, the cream and pink painted villas and above all, her favourite hotel in the whole world.

She had been coming to the Hotel Nettuno for years. She had discovered it by accident one year when she booked a late deal where the hotel was allocated at the last minute. Her room that year had over-looked the car park. From there she watched the rain come down in torrents as a thunderstorm boomed over the lake. When it rains on Lake Garda it pours, but it is quickly over and then the sunshine betrays no hint of the storm that went before. Later that evening she had gone down to a luscious dinner and made friends with the staff. Yes, friends – she was now greeted each year with "Oh you're back!" as they rushed to greet her. It was almost like staying with family. She would watch in admiration as Maitre D' Loris orchestrated his finely tuned dining room. Not a fork out of place, everyone exactly where they should be, every guest attended to with absolute precision while he chatted to them, choosing the perfect wine – he could tell your taste before you had even sat down – suggesting the meals that would tempt your palate most and making sure that everyone felt they had his personal attention. He never seemed to rush, always seemed at ease and everyone left glowing with delight at the end of their meal. She sometimes thought that Loris knew what people wanted better than they knew themselves.

The coach turned off from the wide main road and began to negotiate the twists and turns of the road around the lake. Its sky blue water shimmered under the sun. The road curved, the hotel came into view, with the familiar fruit stall on the edge of the roundabout. She had a sudden craving for watermelon. The breaks hissed, the doors opened, the driver got out to open the luggage hatches. With a deep sigh of contentment she took up her case and walked into the cool air of the hotel. The receptionist beamed. Outside on the terrace couples sipped their drinks and admired the view. All was exactly as it should be.

"Ah Signora Jones – it is good to see you again!"

"And it is very very good to see you again. How is everyone?"

She handed over her passport, filled in the paperwork and collected her key.

"We are all very well. Enjoy your stay."

"Grazie. I shall."

She took the lift to the third floor, turned left and headed down the corridor. She opened the door, set down her case and threw back the curtains to look at the lake. Downstairs people were swimming in the pool, the water looked inviting. It had been a long journey. A quick shower was what was needed, then a stroll into the town to buy some water – but first she had to unpack. Forty five minutes later she walked on to the terrace nodding acknowledgement to the waitress and walked down the steps to the small gate which led onto the lake shore. The gentle breeze ruffled her hair, children were feeding the swans, adults were swimming and sunbathing. A duck came up to her hopefully. She smiled.

"Not yet, little one. On the way back when I have bought some bread." The warmth of the sun was intoxicating. Past the hall, the lawn, the park – the fountain a few hundred yards into the lake sending soft beads of cooling water out – already she could see the brightly painted fishing boats of the harbour, the people sitting out on the piazza eating the luxurious Italian ice cream and sipping at long cold drinks. She sat down at one of the tables. The waiter came over smiling.

"Desidera?"

"Delle olive, acqua minrale per favore"

He nodded and returns a few minutes later with a long glass of iced water and a selection of juicy olives. Bliss – and just what she needed after the journey. The language of Italy had come easily to Diana. Her grandparents had come to Wales as children from the small town of Bardi in North West Italy in the 1920s. They had worked in the Italian cafes of the Rhondda Valley for other Italians from the same town. Later they set up their own café, where Diana's mother still worked. It did the best fish and chips in the valley. Her mother had a smattering of Italian but as she had married a local boy, this hadn't been passed on to her own children. Diana had loved to sit on her grandmother's knee and listened to her soft lullabies. So it was to Italy that she had fled fifteen years ago when her life fell apart. She was then in the last year of university. Her whole future was mapped out before her. She would complete her finals in two days' time, and then in two weeks she was marrying her long term boyfriend Aled. She had been excited and content. Then, on that awful night, she came home to find Aled waiting for her. He had been tense for some weeks. Diana had presumed this was due to the stress of the coming wedding and the assessments he was undergoing as his first year as a teacher came to an end. He stood up as he saw her coming in. Then, calmly and almost without emotion he had told her that the wedding was off and that he had set up house with her former flat-mate Jenny. What happened next was a blur. She cried for days, weeks, months. There was no way that she could sit her final examinations. She lost weight and wouldn't leave her room at her parent's house. Finally her mother persuaded her to see a doctor. It was a slow, painful recovery. As soon as she felt strong enough she set off for Italy, touring the cities then making her way up the Apennine Mountains to Bardi to see long lost relatives. She worked in a bar in Verona for a year then headed back home. She seemed to everyone to have healed; she was almost her old self. Almost. Never again would she let a man break her heart. Never again would she let anyone get close enough.

That was all in the past. She sat watching the world go by just soaking in the atmosphere and the warmth of the sunshine. Then wandered through the narrow streets – nothing had changed, brightly coloured garments dangled outside shops, the inviting smell of olive breads wafted from each corner, everywhere was so full of life yet taken at a leisurely pace. She bought water and her favourite amaretti biscuits from the little shop half way up Borgo Garibaldi. The staff at "La Rocca" knew her well by now. Turning up the hill she walked up to the old church at San Severo. She entered the church, letting her eyes adjust to the darkness. This was a simple place of worship, not ornate like the bigger church on the piazza lower down the town. It was decked with 13th century frescos and the cave like crypt was said to be centuries older. A woman she half recognised was sitting at the back of the church. Nodding to her, she lit a candle, placing coins in the box under the wooden statue of the virgin then sat quietly with her thoughts. A family came in, children chattering. Diana came back to herself, gathered herself and headed back out into the sunshine. She wandered back towards the harbour down a grey stone street illuminated by brightly coloured oil paintings. Stepping in to one of the galleries she noticed a tall handsome man admiring one of the artworks. It was a harbour scene, blue sky, vivid fishing boats and azure water – capturing the essence of the village perfectly. If she could have afforded it she might have bought it herself. He spoke to the gallery manager in fluent Italian, but with a trace of an accent. British possibly? His dress was pure European, casual but smart with more flair than usually found on the streets of Britain, beige linen trousers teamed with a well cut short sleeved shirt. He had an air of understated elegance about him. Diana pulled herself out of her thoughts and strolled back along the lakeside to the hotel to get ready for dinner.

Eight o'clock and she headed downstairs once more. Her long dress swished as she entered the restaurant. Loris was at the door, immaculate as usual. His face lit up as she came towards him. He never forgot a guest. They chatted as he took her to her table and advised on tonight's menu.

"Ah, you see, this corner of the restaurant is more beautiful tonight because you are here."

She giggled despite herself. Ah, Loris! He knew just exactly how much to joke with each guest.

"Tonight, for you, I suggest the pasta with asparagus, yes?"

She nodded. He was always right.

"And for the main course... the salmon trout?"

"Yes please. That sounds lovely."

"And wine? Red or white?"

"Red please."

"How you like your red? Full bodied but smooth?"

"Yes, that would be perfect."

"I will find something for you. And a bottle of water?"

"Yes please."

"You want the water like me or like you?"

She laughed "Sparkling like you!"

"Ah, you remember!"

He laughed. Diana smiled to herself as she watched him interacting with the guests. Joking with the couple on the table behind her, telling them he would charge their wine to the next table. Both couples were laughing now. This did not feel like a formal restaurant, more like a family party. Yet in another corner he was formal and ultra-polite to meet the differing needs of another guest. How well he judged people. How quickly he worked out exactly what their needs were. She went to the buffet table to get some salad.

As she sat down, out of the corner of her eye she noticed a tall figure near the entrance. It was the man from the art gallery. For some inexplicable reason her heart skipped a beat as she watched Loris lead him over to the vacant table next to her. The arrangement in the hotel was that guests selected their food for the evening at breakfast, so the fact that he did not have a menu told Diana that he could not have arrived that day. He smiled at her. She smiled back. He leaned over. Loris turned towards her.

"Diana, this is Mark, an old friend."

She could feel herself blushing.

"Mark, this is Diana, also an old friend."

She nodded at Mark and he returned her acknowledgment with a warm smile. Diana was alarmed at the way her heart was racing. She had not felt attracted to someone like this for years. Words failed her. For goodness sake, she thought, pull yourself together – you're a grown woman, not a schoolgirl.

Relief arrived as Cinzia brought the wine. She opened the bottle doing that special little trick that good waiters have where the top of the seal is cleverly cut so that the wine is kept for the following day. Diana had tried in vain to achieve this herself. She watched Cinzia carefully, but the action was so quick and well-practiced that she again failed to see just how it was done. She poured some into the glass, swirled it around and passed it to her. Diana tasted it.

"That's lovely Cinzia. Thank you. How are you? I have missed you all."

Her blonde curls bobbed as she tossed her head.

"Ah, thank you. I am well. And you?"

"Very well, now that I am here!"

Cinzia poured the water and went off to get the starter.

She was aware of eyes on her and looked up. Mark was still smiling.

"Did you arrive today?"

"Yes, just after lunch. You?"

"On Tuesday. I would gather that it is not your first time in Bardolino."

She laughed.

"Good gracious no! I've been coming here for years."

The smile became a grin.

"Ah, you're a regular like myself then. I love this place. Good food, the best service in Italy –"

"And it is like coming to see old friends!" she finished for him.

"Yes, yes that is it exactly. That is why so many people here come back year after year. I take another holiday at some point during the year but always come here at least once. It rests my soul."

Diana's eyed brightened. Here was a kindred soul. They chatted through the fish course, laughed through the main course and by dessert they realised that they really did have an awful lot in common. As they decided to stroll along the lakeside to one of the cafes to listen to the singing outside the church Diana looked up and noticed Loris smiling. They both caught his eye and laughed.

Mark had found the hotel by accident too. He had run here some years ago, trying to get over the death of his young wife. Loris watched them as they left, walking along the broad pathway along the lake. Leaving the hotel, next to the Centro Nautica they strolled in the moonlight up towards the park. They paused on the point – the Punta Cornicello, listening to the songs and the strumming of the guitars. The moon was reflected in the gentle ripples of the water, ducks laughed at each other, moorhens busied themselves amongst the reeds.

Then they walked past the fountain in the lake and the huge anchor to the harbour and then up to the main square where seats were being laid out for tonight's concert. Every week the choir and orchestra performed on the steps of the church. The concerts were free but there was always a collection for a local charity, followed by home-made cakes in the hall. Again, this was like a family party. Mark and Diana managed to get a table at the Café Central and ordered drinks. The water came back carrying two long orange drinks – Spritz con Aperol. Long, cool, orange, slightly bitter and very refreshing. The square was filling up now. The orchestra took their seats; the choir took up their places on the steps. The crowd cheered, the leader of the orchestra gave the announcements in Italian, German and English, everyone clapped as the conductor appeared and the concert began. Everyone stood for the Italian National anthem. Here the anthem comes first, not at the end as in concerts in Britain. The soloists performed, Puccini, Verdi – and even a bit of Andrew Lloyd Webber! They finished with the whole crowd singing "Foniculi Foniculá" with everyone on their feet clapping and singing. As the performers went back into the hall many of the crowd followed for cake and a chat, others faded into nearby streets where the shops were still open.

Diana and Mark made their way along the Via le Dante Alighieri. Mark told her how he had put his life on hold for the last twelve years since the death of his young wife and their unborn child in a road accident. He had not had a girlfriend since; his heart had not been ready. As they looked into each other's eyes under the warm Italian moonlight they each began to feel that perhaps their hearts were now ready to try again. They said goodnight on the marble staircase and Diana hardly slept waiting to see him again at breakfast. He waited for her at the door to the terrace and they sat together shyly sharing this new experience. Loris leaned over the small wall and picked a blossom from the geraniums in the flower border. He set it on the table beside her.

"For you." he said, then turning to Mark

"No flower for you."

They laughed. They spent the day together walking along the swirling patterns of stone along the lake to the walled town of Lazise, eating lunch inside the castle walls then calling into the Olive museum in Cisano. Then Mark took her up the hill to the wine museum where they bought local wines and took in the breath-taking views across the lake. Then down to Bardolino once more to eat soft cool ice cream at the Yacht bar before walking back along the lake.

They sat together at dinner. Mark seemed pensive,

"Diana, is this just a holiday romance for you or something deeper?"

Diana swallowed hard.

"I have never had a holiday romance. I guess this will be what it will be."

"It's just that..... I think..... I feel…. That is… I'm falling in love with you."

Tears of joy began to brim over her eyes. Thank goodness for waterproof mascara!

"I feel the same way. I never expected to. I never thought I would feel this way about anyone ever again."

They smiled at each other, both of them sensing that this was something special.

And a year later when they returned on their honeymoon they were still smiling. The perfect Maître D had found them both the perfect partner.

The Bardolino Suite

The Safe Option

The Safe Option

The soft spring sun shone down on the centuries old walls of the town as the ferry docked. Barbara moved into the shadow cast by one of the square towers. She gazed up at the solid Sgaligeri architecture. This town still had the feel of the Middle Ages about it despite the scooters which whizzed past. Like many places on the lake, Lazise had been inhabited since Roman times. Maybe that was what brought her back to the lake year after year – the perfect place to indulge her passions – history, languages, and wildlife. But she would have to hurry if she was to catch the ferry back to Bardolino. The hexagonal tower of San Nicoló kept watch over the brightly coloured fishing fleet. She gathered her shopping and walked across the boardway onto the boat, showing her return ticket to the uniformed man on the boat. She made her way upstairs and chose an outside seat to give her a good view of the lakeside towns. The purring of the engine became a roar as the boat turned and chugged out into the deeper water. Ducks quacked as they moved out of the way. Ripples spread out from the boat and ran ashore in gentle waves. She adjusted her hat to shield her eyes from the sun. The people walking along the path next to the lake became smaller and smaller. Warm rays bathed her skin, the sights and sounds of the lake enveloped her. Everything was just as it should be – almost.

The campsites along the lake shore were busy with families, some sunbathing, others queuing for food from the lakeside cafes, and yet more swimming in the clear warm water. Many of them had come for the Easter break and would be gone in a few days. This was her favourite time of year to come to the lake. Almost everyone was Italian, Austrian or German – she thought that she might be the lone Brit in the hotel this week. The tour operators wouldn't be ferrying in coach loads of tourists eager for their two weeks in the sun for another month. The cooler weather meant it was easier for her to walk further and she loved Bardolino at Easter. The only thing that had kept her sane over the last few months was the thought of savouring the culture and cuisine of Lake Garda. It was her favourite part of Italy. She fell in love with the Lake as soon as she saw it, many years ago now and as for Bardolino – if a person didn't fall in love with the pretty fishing town, Barbara felt that they couldn't have a heart to fall in love with. Perhaps it was the easy option for her, coming back to the same place year after year, but that was her style. Her parents had urged her to take the safe option – going to university and securing a "safe" job. As the good daughter that she had always been, she did as they advised and to be fair it had all worked out very well. She got a first class honours degree in European Languages, went on to do her Masters and then secured a position as a lecturer in a fairly good university. She had relished it at first, but over the past few years the students seemed to have become more jaded. Sometimes she wondered why some of them were there – they didn't seem to have much interest in the course. There were days – weeks even, when she felt she was just going through the motions. It did, however, pay the bills – and leave her free to holiday at Easter and the summer. She sat, watching the world go by, the soft spray cooling her face, flying up as the bow of the ferry sped across the water.

Soon they pulled into the next town, Cisano. She recalled walking along the lakeside last summer, beside the huge camp sites. This was where the Italians spent their holidays. There lay the sun worshippers, roasting like nuts on towels and sunbeds. In the reed beds ducks and moorhens gathered their chicks whilst the swans glided by serenely. She remembered calling into the Olive Oil museum – the place was almost like home to her.

The first time she had come to the lake she had travelled by bus. At one time it wasn't possible to circumnavigate the lake by road, but thanks to Mussolini the road now went all around the lake, from the south at Peschera with its ancient walls, up to Riva in the north, where the lake grew thinner and the air colder. From Riva the road passed through arched tunnels to Limone with its disused lemon groves and down to Salo – the resort for the fashionable jet setters. From Salo the road went down to the fortified town of Sirmione – where she had enjoyed many a delightful afternoon. The castle there looked more like something that Walt Disney had dreamed up than anything you would see in a film. Barbara loved it all. It was her lake and the only place in the world she truly felt that she belonged.

Finally the ferry docked in her beloved Bardolino, with its pretty painted fishing boats bobbing busily in the harbour. She paused to watch a pair of crested grebes nodding and bobbing at each other in their courting dance.

All the birds on the lake seemed to be looking for a mate. The seagulls chased each other in noisy tight circles. Swans mirrored each other and made elegant heart shapes with their necks. She had never seen so many different ducks – mallards, tufted ducks, the chestnut headed pochard and its red crested cousin. Moorhens, bitterns and coots busied themselves in the reed beds. A lone cormorant stood like a statue on a pole. Her favourites were the grebes – so many varieties – the great crested with its punk hairdo and a face that gave it a permanent air of self-satisfaction; the little grebe that looked like a cross between a grebe and a duck; and the black necked grebes that looked as if they had been in a tumble dryer. The first time she had seen one diving under water and emerging with an impossibly large fish in its beak she could hardly believe her eyes. Under the clear water she had watched as it swam. They were such improbable creatures as they bobbed up and down, shaking their heads. Aware of the time she roused herself. It was a short walk to the hotel which was her habitual home for the week of her stay The Hotel Nettuno was on the lake front, which gave a spectacular view of the sunset as it painted the lake golden pink before the sun sank down behind the mountains. She opened the small gate at the foot of the garden and walked up the steps to the terrace, waving to the staff as she entered the cool air of the bar. Having collected her key she walked up the swirling marble staircase to her room and prepared for dinner.

Tonight was the Gala Dinner at the hotel – a chance to sample the specialities of the area, to live a life of privilege for a few hours and to forget about her troubles. She took a glass of something orange and sweet from the smiling waitress and selected her canapés. A chorus of ducks quacked their jealousy as they filed past. Barbara smiled as she watched them. Everyone on the lake always seemed to be happy – even the ducks! She had her usual table and was immediately greeted by Loris, the Maître D'. They were old friends by now. Smooth as Como silk, as sparkling as Prosecco, Loris captained the restaurant with a unique blend of authority and charm. His able First Mate Cinzia added to the welcoming atmosphere where friendliness was tempered with respect. They made a formidable team. Many of the diners were "regulars" –coming back to the hotel year after year – as she did herself. Solitary dining could be a mournful experience, but here, she never felt alone. She put her troubles to one side and enjoyed the evening.

She got up rather later than planned the next morning. She would give herself a lazy day – perhaps a short walk into the town, perhaps lunch on the terrace at the hotel. She decided to walk along the back street rather than the lake front this morning. The sunshine seemed borrowed from summer for a few days. Tomorrow she would head north to see the waterfalls near Riva. But, breakfast first – she would have to hurry. As she put away her things ready to leave her room a muted "ping" came from her phone. She glanced at it, irritated. Then she put the phone in the safe and locked the door. Holidays were for forgetting your troubles and enjoying yourself.

A smiling Loris directed her to her breakfast table. She chatted briefly, aware that she was more subdued than usual this morning. This would not do – everyone was doing their best to make her stay wonderful – the least she could do was be cheerful in return. She finished her fruit and waved as she left. "Ciao!" Outside the streets were already busy. A mother passed with her child in a push chair and small dog racing to keep up. His little legs were almost a blur as he valiantly kept pace. Cyclists hurtled past ringing their bells as a warning. The road train stopped to pick up an elderly couple. Avoiding the crowds, Barbara turned up the hill and made for the little church at the top of the town. This was her favourite among the many beautiful churches on the lake. Its simplicity always touched her. She opened the door, allowing her eyes to adjust to the semi-darkness. Soon the church would stand bare and in almost darkness – its altar bare until Easter Sunday. The cave like crypt here was always a source of wonderment to her. She could imagine early Christians centuries ago worshipping here. How many prayers had been answered? How many had knelt quietly here as that deep peace came over them? How many hearts had been lifted? This church had seen the joy of new parents, the restless exuberance of children, the first glimmers of love, the vows of marriage, the pride of grandparents and the sorrow of their passing. Life's dramas had been played out here for more than twelve centuries. Then suddenly, it all became too much. Her stifled sobs echoed in the semi-darkness as tears flowed freely down her face. In the depths of her despair she felt a calm reassurance that all would be well. The door opened with a click and a creak. A young woman came in, moving to light a candle. Barbara hurried out. She felt much calmer now, but was anxious that no one would see the bloodshot eyes and blotchy face which betrayed her predicament. She blinked in the brilliant sunshine and made her way through the narrow lanes to the Via D'Alghiera so that she could come into the hotel by the road entrance, rather than the walk along the busy lake side. The receptionist looked worried as she gave her key. Loris was busy as she made her way towards the stairs, but he looked up as she passed – his eyes questioning.

She washed her face. Right. There was no point in feeling sorry for herself. She was still on holiday and she was determined to enjoy herself. She chose her prettiest dress, redid her make-up and went down to have lunch.

Sitting on the sunbathed terrace she ordered a bottle of sparkling water and perused the menu. The sun was reflected in the rippling lake, a line of ducks quacked noisily. She sighed. She was in Bardolino – the happiest town in Italy according to statistics she had read somewhere. If a miracle could happen anywhere it would be here. Loris came over to her

"Is everything ok?

"Yes, I had a bad headache earlier – I'm fine now."

She smiled weakly. He knew her well enough to detect the lie. She ordered a large salad.

When he returned she hesitated for a moment, then ventured

"May I ask you a question?"

"Of course, but if you are going to ask me to marry you I must tell you that my girlfriend would not be happy…."

She laughed. How did his girlfriend cope with his crazy sense of humour? They must be well suited, she thought.

"You are contented with your life. It's obvious. What is the secret?"

He tilted his head to one side.

"You know, I always say to my girlfriend, a person is happiest when he is doing something he loves."

She nodded.

"Yes, there is more to life than money. "

Before she had chance to continue he was called back to the dining room. There was wisdom there, she thought.

After lunch she sat on a bench by the lake. The town had shut down for lunch. The air was warm and everything was still apart from the gentle lapping of the water. There was nowhere else she would rather be. The trees were decked with painted yoghurt pots, each bearing the name of the child who had made it. How typical of the place, that even the clumsiest attempts at artwork were valued for their effort. How did this small town, with its choir and orchestra keep such a sense of community despite being swamped by tourists for half of the year? What was the magic that seeped from the geothermal vents in the lake, tempering its climate? Was this what gave the oil its flavour and the wine its depth? There was something very special about the place.

After breakfast the next morning she caught the bus to the north end of the lake. This was a first for her. Usually she got the ferry up to Malcésine, either to get the cable car to the top of Monte Baldo for the stunning views of the lake and the snow-capped peaks, or climbed up the seemingly never ending steps to the top of the magnificent castle to look out over the lake at the bright sails of the windsurfers below. Today, she would go to Riva and then try to find her way to the famous waterfalls. Loris had told her about them – he was better than any guide book! There were no trips from the hotel, but she was more than confident enough here to get the bus. The lake looks rather like a misshapen golf club, wider in the south then tapering as it stretches northward. Barbara noted the changes as the bus trundled along. First to the bustling town of Garda, full of colour where the town was flat, then on through Torri, its castle guarding the neck of the lake. As they neared Brenzone the valley narrowed further, houses clinging to the steep sides of the mountains and the road running right up against the lake edge. Most of the people on the bus got off at Malcésine. A lady in her sixties dressed in fake leopard skin, high heels and more jewellery than Barbara could afford to insure got on the bus and sat behind her. Two seconds later she was having an animated conversation loud enough for the whole bus to hear. The cause of her anxiety seemed to be the family dinner and the arrival of said family from various places. Barbara did her best not to listen, trying to concentrate on the changing scenery as the mountainsides became steeper and the scattered houses seemed to defy gravity. The leopard lady got off the bus at Tórbale, patting her lacquered hair into place as she did so. Finally the bus circumnavigated the town to pull into the bus station at Riva. She asked the driver for directions up to the waterfalls. It was possible to get a bus but as it was a sunny day she decided to walk. The Cascata del Verone was well sign posted – about three kilometres up the mountain road. She walked alongside the tennis courts and then crossed the road to head up the slope. Every so often she paused to admire the scene of Riva del Garda laid out below, with its colourful hotels and restaurants. It was quite a hike up the mountainside, and she rather regretted not waiting for the bus. The waterfalls were worth it though. The cascade down the gorge was almost deafening and when she entered the upper cavern the force of the water was breath taking. The fine spray soaked her as she leaned to get a better look. A Japanese couple were videoing everything. She offered to take their picture with the waterfall as the backdrop – they smiled their delight. Deciding to save her feet she got the bus back down the mountain and had lunch in the town. The northern end of the lake is colder than the south and the wind can whip through the square in Riva. She decided to eat indoors, despite the sunshine. After lunch she browsed the shops then caught the bus back to Bardolino.

It began to drizzle. As the view was obscured she had time to brood on her thoughts. The conversation she had had with Loris came back to her. Things had been far from ideal at work for some time, but since Christmas things had become very strained and much as she tried to ignore it, it was clear that something bad was in the offing. The last but one day before the end of term she had a message to see her boss. He was looking very stern.

Barbara, I have some bad news, I'm afraid"

She looked up. What now? They had cut the departmental budgets so much already, how could they possibly cut more?

"The board has decided to axe the Modern Languages degree from September."

She couldn't believe her ears.

"What? What about the people who are expecting to start the course in September? What about the students who are part way through?"

"We have sent letters to the students. They will be offered alternative degrees with language modules. There weren't many of them, anyway."

"But what if they don't want to do that?

"They will have to complete their studies elsewhere"

This was madness. She doubted that the students would have time to make other arrangements. How many lives would be turned upside down? Her protests fell on deaf ears. It was clear that this decision had been taken some time ago and that the students were not the main consideration. But there was more to come

"As a result we won't need two full time members of staff for languages..."

"What are you trying to say?"

"Of course, we shall pay you until the end of August."

She had thought her world was at an end. She would, of course, have time to find something at another university, but as she knew already, many universities were simply not recruiting due to budget cuts. She had assumed that she would find something but somehow the thought just made her feel weary. There was, as she had said, more to life than money. Here, on the lake she had felt alive once more and the thought of going back to academia just filled her with dread. Why couldn't she stay here, in the place she loved? What a foolish idea! But was it? What would she do? She could teach – she did have qualifications to teach English as a second language, but would that be jumping out the frying pan and into the fire? If this was her chance to do something that she really wanted to do, what would that be? She had always dreamed of writing, novels, travelogues – poetry even. She had always written – felt compelled to even – but there had never been the time to do it seriously. She knew it wasn't something that she could make a good living from doing. Could she find something to do part time here and use the rest of the time to write? She had a house – perhaps she could rent it out to give herself a steady income to at least cover the rent of a flat here and perhaps even go part way to paying some of her other bills. She had a fair bit of local knowledge. Could she put this to good use?

The next day was Good Friday. She took the ferry over to Gardone – again on the recommendation of the Maître D. There was a small road train which wound up the hill and passed the Heller Botanical Gardens – the reason for her visit. The flowers were indeed, beautiful – and interspersed with quirky modern sculptures. In the centre of the gardens was a mini mountain. Barbara couldn't tell if it was natural or man-made. Brown lizards basked on the stones – fleeing quickly as soon as a human got close. Their movements were so swift. They seemed to know exactly when to run and hide. Barbara reflected that for all their intellect human beings seemed to be far less able to make sensible decisions. Her head told her to go home and get another soulless job teaching students who cared more about their social life than having any real passion for the course. Her heart was screaming that she should stay here, live on less and find something to do that made her feel life was actually worth living. Which would win?

The next morning she went down to the market in Bardolino. She loved the Easter market. In front of her was a stall selling what looked at first glance to be slices of melon, shellfish and fruit. It was only when you looked very closely that you could tell that they were all made from marzipan. She bought a few dainty pieces to take home. Standing next to her was a rather pale looking woman. As she moved away from the stall she seemed to miss her footing. Barbara caught her arm to stop her from falling.

"Are you ok?"

"Yes, thank you. I just need to sit down"

Barbara gently led the woman over to a nearby bench.

"Would you like some water?"

The woman nodded. Barbara had an unopened bottle of water in her bag, which she passed to her companion. Slowly the colour returned to her cheeks.

"Are you on holiday?" Barbara wondered if she perhaps lived nearby. She didn't look well enough to go far.

"No. I am from Bardolino."

"Lucky you! There is so much community here. I love the decorated trees!"

The woman smiled "Yes, the children always get so excited about it. My daughter has brought everyone in the family to see the tree her class did!"

They chatted for a few minutes. The conversation was proving enlightening. Just then, a young girl and a man in his thirties came towards them.

"Mama!" The girl was eager to show what she had bought. It was a beautiful Easter candle.

Barbara made her way back to the hotel to pack. She was returning home that evening. There was a lot to think about.

Less than two months later it was all arranged. She found someone to rent her house giving her an income which was considerably more than the rent on the one bedroom apartment she leased for a year in Cisano. She took a job at a local school, covering the maternity leave for the woman she had met at the Easter market. And in her spare time she wrote. The words flowed as easily as the waters of the river Mincio now that she was in the land of her inspiration. She felt so at home.

One day, some months later, she called in to see her friends at the hotel where all her happiness had begun. Sitting on the terrace she asked Loris for his recommendation.

"How are you finding your new life?"

"I am completely happy. The children are so full of enthusiasm. It is a pleasure to teach them. I feel as though I have found myself."

"I am glad."

"If I hadn't taken your advice, I wouldn't be here you know."

"My advice? What did I say?"

"You said that the key to happiness was to do what you love doing."

"Oh, you should never listen to me!"

"I'm very glad that I did."

"What will you do when the contract ends?"

"I have another contract lined up for a year. And I have begun writing a book. This place inspires me."

"A book? About the history?"

"The history, the geology, the beauty – and about finding yourself."

As she walked back along the lake front the sun was painting the lake a soft pink.

The people of the happiest town in Italy were getting ready for another musical concert. Perhaps it is the air, perhaps it is the food….but perhaps it is the magic of the lake. For wonderful things surely happen in Bardolino.

The End

For further information about this author and her other books, visit www.helenaileendavies.com